ida,
ALWAYS

For Eddie and Elsie, and
Carl and Margaret,
who are together and with me,
always.

Special thanks to my incredible
editor, Emma Ledbetter,
for wondering over every word
with me; to Namrata Tripathi, for
welcoming these bears; and to
Adah Nuchi, for sparking the story.
—C. L.

For my grandmas and grandpas
—C. S.

ATHENEUM BOOKS FOR YOUNG READERS • An imprint of Simon & Schuster Children's Publishing Division • 1230 Avenue of the Americas, New York, New York 10020 • Text copyright © 2016 by Caron Levis • Illustrations copyright © 2016 by Charles Santoso • All rights reserved, including the right of reproduction in whole or in part in any form. • ATHENEUM BOOKS FOR YOUNG READERS is a registered trademark of Simon & Schuster, Inc. • Atheneum logo is a trademark of Simon & Schuster, Inc. • For information about special discounts for bulk purchases, please contact Simon & Schuster Special Sales at 1-866-506-1949 or business@simonandschuster.com. • The Simon & Schuster Speakers Bureau can bring authors to your live event. For more information or to book an event, contact the Simon & Schuster Speakers Bureau at 1-866-248-3049 or visit our website at www.simonspeakers.com. • Book design by Ann Bobco • The text for this book is set in Bodoni Old Face BE. • The illustrations for this book are digitally rendered. • Manufactured in China • 0619 SCP • 10 9 8 7 • Library of Congress Cataloging-in-Publication Data • Levis, Caron. • Ida, always / written by Caron Levis ; illustrated by Charles Santoso. — First edition. • pages cm • Summary: A polar bear grieves over the loss of his companion, based on the real-life Gus and Ida of New York's Central Park Zoo. • ISBN 978-1-4814-2640-4 • ISBN 978-1-4814-2641-1 (eBook) • 1. Polar bear—Juvenile fiction. [1. Polar bear—Fiction. 2. Best friends—Fiction. 3. Friendship—Fiction. 4. Grief—Fiction. 5. Loss (Psychology)—Fiction. 6. Central Park (New York,

ida,
ALWAYS

CARON LEVIS and **CHARLES SANTOSO**

A̶ ATHENEUM BOOKS FOR YOUNG READERS

New York
London
Toronto
Sydney
New Delhi

Gus lived in a big park in the middle of an even bigger city.
Buildings grew around him and shifted the shape of the sky.
Zookeepers poked in and out. Visitors came and went.

But every morning, when keys clicked and shoes clacked,
Gus crawled out of his cave and spent his day with Ida.
Ida was right there. Always.

When Gus tossed the ball, Ida was there to catch it.

And when Gus splashed water,
Ida was there
to splash him right back.

They chased and raced
until school bells rang.

Then the two friends flopped onto their favorite rock
while the city pulsed around them.
"I wish we could see it," Gus sighed.
"You don't have to see it to feel it," said Ida.
"Listen."

They heard buses groan; trucks rumble;
police whistle; taxis honk; pigeons coo;
people say **Hey**, **Wait**, **Yo**, **Hello**;
and children laugh.

"That's the city's heartbeat," said Ida.
"It's right here with us. Always."

When the sky grew dark, Gus and Ida waved good night
and crawled off to their caves.
With the subways humming underground, they added
their snores to the sounds of their city.
Every day was always the same.

Until one morning, when keys clicked and
shoes clacked, Gus crawled out . . .

but Ida wasn't there.
Gus lumbered to Ida's cave.

He heard her breathing, coughing, snoring. Sleeping.

He sat in their
sunniest spot
and waited.

The coffee carts
ground their beans,
and the squirrels
squabbled over crumbs.

Visitors shuffled in.
Keepers bustled about.

Ida had never
slept so late.

Snow monkeys
and taxicabs screeched.
Ice-cream trucks
jingled.

Still
Ida didn't come.

Keeper Sonya came instead.

Sonya told Gus that Ida was very sick.

Usually, there's a way to make a sick bear better,

but this time was different.

Ida wouldn't hurt, but she would get tired

and too weak to swim and play.

Then one day, when her body stopped working,

Ida would die.

Sonya's voice was soft.

But the words felt rough to Gus.
His insides churned. His chin shook.
The sky rumbled.
Gus rushed to his friend.

"Don't go," he growled.
"Don't go,
don't go . . .
DON'T!"

Ida growled right back.

Together they stomped and snarled. Their growls turned into howls
so loud they filled up the zoo, rising higher than skyscrapers,
scaring pigeons, surging toward stars.

And then they stopped.

Two friends folded into one shadow
and slumped quietly on the rocks.

Two bear noses sniffled, two bear breaths panted,
two bear hearts echoed each other's beat.

A plane roared overhead. Gus and Ida wondered where it was going.
They wondered where Ida was going, too.

They wondered and guessed and imagined
as they whispered nose to nose.
"Wherever I go," said Ida, "I bet I'll always smell your fishy breath!"

That made Gus smile. He wasn't sure if he should. But Ida was giggling, too.
They let their laughs bounce back and forth between them.

From then on, Ida spent most days in her cave.
She slept a lot, but she didn't hurt.
The keepers took good care of her.

And Gus helped.
He gathered her favorite toys and fishy treats.
He brought her visitors' notes.

There were growling days

and laughing days

and days that mixed them up.

Sometimes Ida needed a moment alone.

And sometimes Gus did too.

But at the end of each day, Gus always told Ida, "I'll miss you."

And Ida always told Gus, "I'll miss you, too."

They would cuddle until the sky grew dark
and the lamps of the city clicked on.
They would wave good night a thousand times.
Then wave a few times more.

Then one sunny day,

while Gus smoothed her fur,

Ida curled into quiet,

her eyes fluttered shut,

and they didn't open anymore.

Gus pressed one last pat into Ida's paw.

The papers shared the news.
The city cried. For days the zoo was filled with good-byes.

The News
GOOD-BYE, IDA

Now when keys click and shoes clack,
Gus crawls out of his cave
knowing Ida won't be there.

He dives and swims alone,

and he eats his lunch
with Sonya.

They roll
Ida's favorite
yellow ball.

Some days Gus forgets. He looks for Ida
on the rock, in her cave, behind the waterfall.
When he remembers she isn't there,
he rests in the shadows.

But even in the shadows,
the sounds of the city reach him.
He hears buses groan; trucks rumble;
police whistle; taxis honk; pigeons coo;
people say **Hey**, **Wait**, **Yo**, **Hello**;
and children laugh.

Gus smiles.

He steps into the spot
where Ida liked to soak in the sun.
He listens to their city pulsing around him.

He remembers that Ida said
you don't have to see it to feel it.

The sidewalks tap and the streets hum.
Gus's heart beats.

And Ida is right there.

Always.

Author's Note

Ida, Always is a fictional story inspired by the real pair of polar bears, Ida and Gus, who lived together in New York City's Central Park Zoo. The two bears swam, played, and cuddled together for many years. They were visited by more than twenty million people from all over the world and deeply cared for by their zookeepers. By the time Ida became ill and died in 2011, she had created many wonderful memories for friends to remember her by, and when Gus died two years later, friends cherished their many memories of him, too.

While I was working on this story, I visited Gus. He sat on a large rock, surrounded by the city's skyline, with his head tilted toward the sun. Like other loved ones who have passed away, Gus and Ida will be with me, always.

—C. L.